Rude Mule

About Mules

Imagine if a horse and a donkey had a baby. Well, that baby would be called a mule. Mules don't like being made to do anything unless they want to. They're very stubborn creatures, just like some people! But mules are clever and they're easy to train if you treat them kindly. If you ever meet a mule, be sure to be gentle. Then he'll want to be your friend. He'll have lots of fun playing with you. And he'll forget all about being stubborn!

For my friend, David Fenton,
and for my friend, Derek Whitehead.
Thank you for always being such great supporters.
With love – P.D.E.

To the dear Nicolo – B.N.

First published in 2002 by Macmillan Children's Books
A division of Macmillan Publishers Limited
20 New Wharf Road, London N1 9RR
Basingstoke and Oxford
Associated companies throughout the world
www.macmillan.com
This edition produced 2003 for The Book People Ltd,
Hall Wood Avenue, Haydock, St Helens WA11 9UL.

ISBN 0 333 96017 3 HB
ISBN 0 333 96018 1 PB

Text copyright © 2002 Pamela Duncan Edwards
Illustrations copyright © 2002 Barbara Nascimbeni
Moral rights asserted

1 3 5 7 9 8 6 4 2

A CIP catalogue record for this book is available from the British Library.

Printed in Hong Kong

PAMELA DUNCAN EDWARDS

Rude Mule

illustrated by
BARBARA NASCIMBENI

TED SMART

What would you do
if a mule knocked on your door one day
and said, "I've come for lunch"?
You'd say, "Hello! Come in, Mule."

What if he came in and sat down at the table?

You'd say, "Mule, wash your hooves before lunch."

But what if he said, **"won't!"**

You'd say, "No lunch for you, then."

Then what if he brayed a rude mule hee-haw?

You'd ignore him until he stopped, wouldn't you?

What if he got tired of making a fuss and
washed his hooves under the tap politely?
You'd say, "Would you like some spaghetti?"
What if he just said, "Okay."
You'd say, "Mule, say, 'Yes, please'."

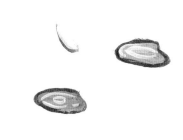

What if he said, "**won't!**"
You'd say, "No spaghetti for you, then."

What if he brayed a rude mule hee-haw
and stamped his four stubborn hooves?
You'd ignore him until he stopped,
wouldn't you?

What if he got tired of making a fuss and said,
"Yes, please," politely?
You'd serve him some spaghetti, wouldn't you?
And what if he began to slurp and gobble?
You'd say, "Mule, eat your food quietly."

But what if he said, "**won't!**"
You'd say, "Then we won't be able to play
with my train set after lunch."

What if he brayed a rude mule hee-haw
and stamped his four stubborn hooves and
blew a loud "plaaah" down his big mule nose?

plaaah!

You'd ignore him until
he stopped, wouldn't you?

What if he got tired of making a fuss
and began to eat quietly?
You'd say, "When we play with my train set,
you can be the driver."

But what if he got very excited
and jumped down from the table?
You'd say, "Mule, say, 'May I leave the table?'"
What if he said, "**won't!**"
You'd say, "Then my train will have to do
without a driver today."

What if he brayed a rude mule hee-haw
and stamped his four stubborn hooves
and blew a loud "plaaah" down his big mule
nose and poked out his red mule tongue?
You'd ignore him until he stopped,
wouldn't you?

What if he got tired of making a fuss
and said, "Please may I leave the table?"
very politely.

Then Mule would get to drive the train.

You'd play hide and seek.

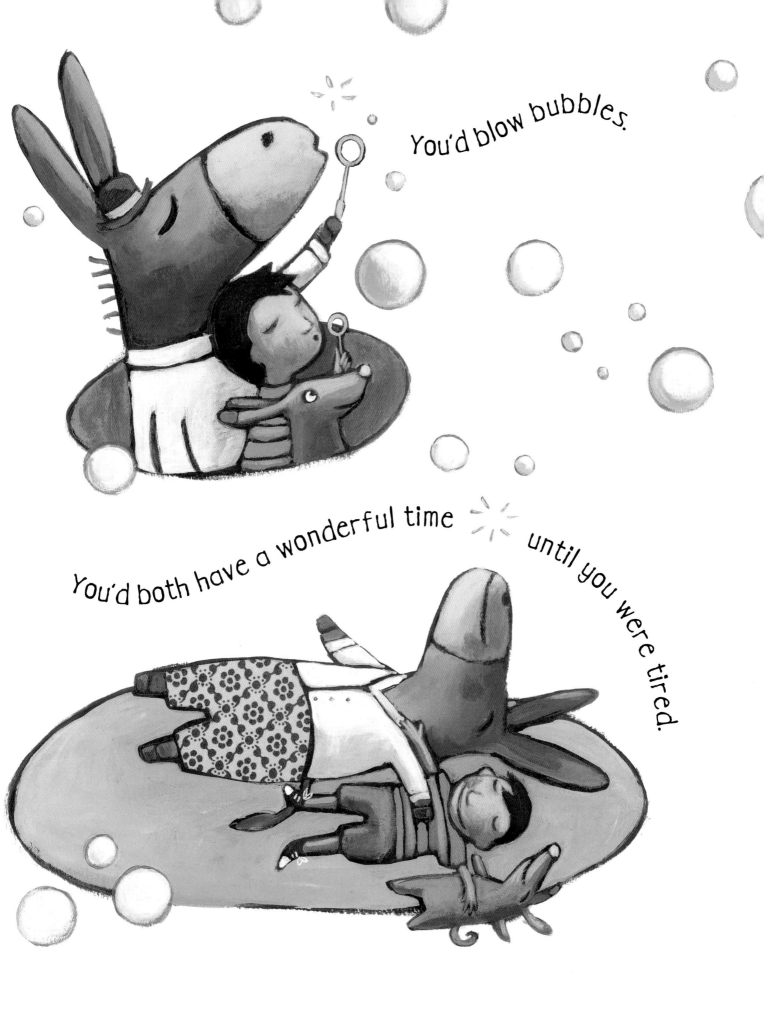

What if he said, "I'm going home now!"
and got ready to leave?
You'd say, "Mule, what should you say now?"
What if he blinked his bright mule eyes
and wrinkled his mule forehead and thought,
and thought?

Then what if he smiled a big toothy mule smile
and said very politely, "Thank you for having me.
I've had a lovely time."
You'd say, "Come again tomorrow and
we'll paddle in my paddling pool."

Then I bet he'd bray
a happy mule hee-haw

and clap his mule hooves
and blow a quiet "plaaah"
down his big mule nose

and lick you gently with his red mule tongue

and give you
a giant mule hug.

Then you'd wave goodbye to him
very politely.

And you'd go and get your paddling pool ready,
wouldn't you?

MACMILLAN CHILDREN'S BOOKS